THE *DIARY OF A WIMPY KID* SERIES

ALSO BY JEFF KINNEY

The Wimpy Kid Do-It-Yourself Book

The Wimpy Kid Movie Diary

The Wimpy Kid Movie Diary: The Next Chapter

Diary of an Awesome Friendly Kid: Rowley Jefferson's Journal

The Wimpy Kid

Do-It-Yourself Book

by Jeff Kinney

YOUR
PICTURE
HERE
↓

AMULET BOOKS

New York

Library of Congress Control Number: 2011904257

ISBN 978-1-4197-4190-6

Book design by Jeff Kinney
Cover design by Jeff Kinney and Chad W. Beckerman
Cover photograph by Geoff Spear
Coloring on last sixteen color comics by Nate Greenwall

Printed and bound in U.S.A.
40 39 38 37 36 35 34 33

Amulet Books are available at special discounts when purchased in quantity for premiums and promotions as well as fundraising or educational use. Special editions can also be created to specification. For details, contact specialsales@abramsbooks.com or the address below.

Amulet Books® is a registered trademark of Harry N. Abrams, Inc.

ABRAMS The Art of Books
195 Broadway, New York, NY 10007
abramsbooks.com

THIS BOOK BELONGS TO:

Ryan and Conor

IF FOUND, PLEASE RETURN
TO THIS ADDRESS:

97 oakland ave

(NO REWARD)

What're you gonna do with this thing?

OK, this is your book now, so technically you can do whatever you want with it.

But if you write anything in this journal, make sure you hold on to it. Because one day you're gonna want to show people what you were like back when you were a kid.

Whatever you do, just make sure you don't write down your "feelings" in here. Because one thing's for sure: This is NOT a diary.

Your DESERT

If you were gonna be marooned for the rest of your life, what would you want to have with you?

Video games

Ryan

1. Fortnite
2. Roblox
3. FNAF

Songs

R

1. Shake
2. Believer
3. Ching Ching hanji

ISLAND picks

Books C

1. Diary of a Wimpy Kid
2. Level up 2017 - 2024
3. Goosebumps

Movies / T.V. Shows

1. Rick and Morty
2. Terminator 2: Judgement Day
3. Gravity Falls.

Have you

Have you ever gotten a haircut that was so bad you needed to stay home from school?

YES ☑ NO ☐

Have you ever had to put suntan lotion on a grown-up?

YES ☐ NO ☑

Have you ever been bitten by an animal?

YES ☑
NO ☐

Have you ever been bitten by a person?

YES ☑
NO ☐

Have you ever tried to blow a bubble with a mouthful of raisins?

YES ☐ NO ☑

EVER...

Have you ever peed in a swimming pool?

YES ☑   NO ☐

Have you ever been kissed full on the lips by a relative who's older than seventy?

YES ☐   NO ☑

Have you ever been sent home early by one of your friends' parents?

YES ☐   NO ☑

Have you ever had to change a diaper?

A LITTLE HELP?

YES ☐   NO ☑

5

PERSONALITY

What's your favorite ANIMAL?

C Lion / monkey
R Rabbit

Write down FOUR ADJECTIVES that describe why you like that animal:

(EXAMPLE: FRIENDLY, COOL, ETC.)

R funny   C fast
fat / smart   intelligent... not

What's your favorite COLOR?

C Blue / Red R

Write down FOUR ADJECTIVES that describe why you like that color:

R Dark   cool R
E light   c cold

The adjectives you wrote down for your favorite ANIMAL
describe HOW YOU THINK OF YOURSELF.
The adjectives you wrote down for your favorite COLOR
describe HOW OTHER PEOPLE THINK OF YOU.

TEST

ANSWER THESE QUESTIONS AND THEN FLIP THE BOOK UPSIDE DOWN TO FIND OUT THINGS YOU NEVER KNEW ABOUT YOURSELF.

What's the title of the last BOOK you read?

The Year Of the Dog

List FOUR ADJECTIVES that describe what you thought of that book:

cool
fun

educational
deep

What's the name of your favorite MOVIE?

Willy Wonka

Rick and morty

Write down FOUR ADJECTIVES that describe why you liked that movie:

warming
Sweet

funny
action

The adjectives you wrote down for the last BOOK you read describe HOW YOU THINK OF SCHOOL. The adjectives you wrote down for your favorite MOVIE describe WHAT YOU'LL BE LIKE in thirty years.

Unfinished

Zoo-Wee Mama!

COMICS

Zoo-Wee Mama!

Make your

OWN comics

Ralphy and Phil

What's in your

BRAIN?

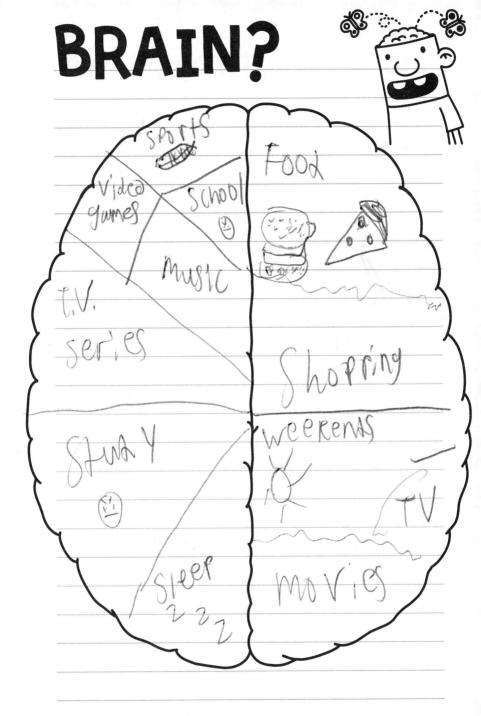

SPORTS

Video games

School

T.V. series

music

FOOD

Shopping

Study

weekends

TV

Sleep
Z Z Z

movies

Predict the

I TOTALLY CALLED IT!

AW, RATS!

I officially predict that twenty years from now cars will run on _electrons_ instead of gasoline. A cheeseburger will cost $ _40_, and a ticket to the movies will cost $ _1000_. Pets will have their own _ball_s. Underwear will be made out of _clay_. _hw/tests_ will no longer exist. A _guy_ named _Jim Hackett_ will be president. There will be more _Aliens_ than people.

The annoying catchphrase will be:
Wabb a lub a dub dub !

WUBBA DUBB, MY TUBB?

RAT-A-TAT-TAT AND CHICKEN FAT!

FUTURE

Aliens will visit our planet in the year __2099__ and make the following announcement:

Halloween should be an off day, but you school peeps didn't listen!

> BROCCOLI WAS NEVER MEANT TO BE EATEN!

> I KNEW IT!

The number-one thing that will get on old people's nerves twenty years from now will be:

People on their long and peeing on it.

> CURSE THOSE FANCY JIMJAMS!

WHIRRRR

Predict the

IN FIFTY YEARS:

Robots and mankind will be locked in a battle for supremacy.   TRUE ☑   FALSE ☐

Parents will be banned from dancing within twenty feet of their children.   TRUE ☑   FALSE ☐

People will have instant-messaging chips implanted in their brains.   TRUE ☑   FALSE ☐

FUTURE

YOUR FIVE BOLD PREDICTIONS FOR THE FUTURE:

1. Get a Job

2. be Successful

3. be an athlete

4. goto a good College

5. earn money.

(WRITE EVERYTHING DOWN NOW
SO YOU CAN TELL YOUR FRIENDS
"I TOLD YOU SO" LATER ON.)

Predict YOUR

Answer these questions, then check back when you're an adult to see how you did!

WHEN I'M 30 YEARS OLD

I will live __10__ miles from my current home.

I will be: MARRIED ☑ SINGLE ☐

I will have __3__ kids and a __Kid__ named _Conor Carrig jr._

I will work as a _athlete_ and make __1,000,000__ dollars a year.

I will live in a _Mansion_ on a _beach_ .

I will take a _train_ to work every day.

future

I will be __6__ feet _____ inches tall.

I will have the same basic haircut
I have now. TRUE ☐   FALSE ☑

I will have the same best friend I have right
now. TRUE ☑   FALSE ☐

I will be in really
excellent shape.
TRUE ☑   FALSE ☐

I will listen to the same kind of music I listen to
now. TRUE ☑   FALSE ☐

I will have visited __5__ different countries.

The thing that will change the most about me
between now and then will be: My voice
and my personality
_____.

Predict YOUR

What you're basically gonna do here is roll a die over and over, crossing off items when you land on them, like this:

1ST ROLL: ⚁

2ND ROLL: ⚀

3RD ROLL: ⚂

HOME:
1 Apartment
2 House
3 ~~Mansion~~
1 Igloo
2

LOCATION:
1 ~~Mountains~~
2 Beach
3 City
~~Iceberg~~

Keep going through the list, and when you get to the end, jump back to the beginning. When there's only one item left in a category, circle it. Once you've got an item in each category circled, you'll know your future! Good luck!

MY LIFE STINKS.

future

HOME:
Apartment
House
~~Mansion~~ (circled)
Igloo

JOB:
Doctor
(Actor) (circled)
Clown
Mechanic
Lawyer
Pilot
(Pro athlete) (circled)
Dentist
Magician
Whatever you want

LOCATION:
Mountains
(Beach) (circled)
City
Iceberg

KIDS:
None
One
(Two) (circled)
Ten

VEHICLE:
(Car) (circled)
Motorcycle
Helicopter
Skateboard

PET:
(Dog) (circled)
Cat
Bird
Turtle

SALARY:
$100 a year
$100,000 a year
$1 million a year
$100 million a year (circled)

Design your

GREG HEFFLEY'S FUTURE HOUSE

ARCADE

BOWLING ALLEY

INDOOR POOL

MASTER BEDROOM

ENTRANCE

90-INCH PLASMA TV

— HOT TUB

PIZZERIA

GO-CART TRACK

SERVANTS' QUARTERS

DREAM HOUSE

Conor and Ryans Dream house

YOUR FUTURE HOUSE

indoor Pool

Storage

Arcade

Bowling alley

indoor mini Mall (all free stuff)

Dining room w/ friends

closet

Nice kitchen

Master bed

Plasma T.V. with multiple gaming consoles

Luxorious bathroom

hot tub

Buffet (all you can eat)

Movie theater

super car garage

Lambo

FRIENDS

Jake

MOST LIKELY TO FALL
ASLEEP IN CLASS

Valery

MOST LIKELY TO FAINT
AT THE SIGHT OF BLOOD

Jungwon

MOST LIKELY TO
BECOME A BILLIONAIRE

Jiha

MOST LIKELY TO BE ON
A REALITY TV SHOW

HALL OF FAME

Brandon

MOST LIKELY TO
BECOME PRESIDENT

MOST LIKELY TO
ACCIDENTALLY WEAR
PAJAMAS TO SCHOOL

MOST LIKELY TO
JOIN THE CIRCUS

MOST LIKELY TO SET
A WORLD RECORD

A few questions

What's the most embarrassing thing that ever happened to someone who wasn't you?

 HEYYY...

What's the worst thing you ever ate?

How many steps does it take you to jump into bed after you turn off the light?

How much would you be willing to pay for an extra hour of sleep in the morning?

$5,000.00

from GREG

Have you ever pretended you were sick so you could stay home from school?

(NEW VIDEO GAME)

Does it get on your nerves when people skip?

Did you ever do something bad that you never got busted for?

Unfinished

Ugly Eugene

COMICS

Ugly Eugene

Make your

OWN comics

Which would you

☐ Sleep in the bathtub
☑ Sleep in your parents' bedroom

☐ Eat the same food at every
meal for the rest of your life
☑ Watch the same TV series for
the rest of your life

☑ Have the power to turn invisible,
but only for ten seconds at a time
☐ Have the power to fly, but only
two feet off the ground

☑ Go without television for a month
☐ Go without the internet for a month

☐ Spend the whole night in a haunted house
☑ Spend one minute in a room full of spiders

☐ Be the main actor in a really bad movie
☑ Have a small part in a really good movie

RATHER DO?

- ☑ Wear the same Halloween costume every year
- ☐ Wear the same pair of socks for a week

GOBBLE *SMACK*

- ☑ Try to sell chocolate bars to your neighbors for a school fundraiser
- ☐ Give up candy for a month

- ☑ Be so famous that everyone knows who you are
- ☐ Live a quiet life and have complete privacy

- ☑ Have the power to predict the future
- ☐ Have the power to see into the past

- ☐ Get a free pass from taking a shower or bath
- ☑ Get a free pass from doing your homework

SOAP

- ☐ Have all of the world's music for free
- ☑ Have all of the world's video games for free

Good advice for

1. Don't use the bathroom on the second floor, because there aren't any stall doors in there.

2. Be careful who you sit next to in the cafeteria.

3. Don't pick your nose right before you get your school picture taken.

next year's class

1.

2.

3.

4.

Draw your FAMILY

the way Greg Heffley would

Draw up your

How many generations can you trace your family history back?

MEEMAW PEEPAW LULU POPPY REMUS GAMMIE WILLIAM HELEN

GRAMMA GRAMPA GRANDPA NANA

MOM DAD

GREG

FAMILY TREE

Create your OWN family tree in the space below!

Your FAVORITES

TV show: Rick and morzy

Band: Guns n Rges

Sports team: 49ers

Food: Burgers/Barbeque

Celebrity:

Smell: body wash smell

Villain: Joker

Shoe brand: jordan

Store: the mall in general

Soda: Coke

Cereal:

Super hero:

Candy:

Restaurant:

Athlete: Micheal Jordan

Game system: PSU

Comic strip:

Magazine: Sports illustrated

Car: Lamboghini

Your LEAST favorites

TV show:

Band:

Sports team:

Food:

Celebrity:

Smell:

Villain:

Shoe brand:

Store:

Soda:

Cereal:

Super hero:

Candy:

Restaurant:

Athlete:

Game system:

Comic strip:

Magazine:

Car:

Record your

BEST DREAM

BEST PHOTO

BEST ATHLETIC FEAT

FINEST MOMENTS

FUNNIEST QUOTE

COOLEST AWARD

BEST HALLOWEEN COSTUME

BEST MEAL

Things you should do

☐ Stay up all night.

☐ Ride on a roller coaster with a loop in it.

☐ Get in a food fight. THWAP

☐ Get an autograph from a famous person.

☐ Get a hole in one in miniature golf.

☐ Give yourself a haircut.

☐ Write down an idea for an invention.

☐ Spend three nights in a row away from home.

☐ Mail someone a letter with a real stamp and everything.

Dear Gramma, Please send money.

I ONLY HAVE A FEW MORE TO GO!

before you get old

☐ Go on a campout.

zzz

☐ Read a whole book with no pictures in it.

?

☐ Beat someone who's older than you in a footrace.

☐ Make it through a whole lollipop without biting it.

☐ Use a porta-potty.

KNOCK KNOCK

OCCUPIED!

☐ Score at least one point in an organized sport.

☐ Try out for a talent show.

EH?

Make your own
TIME CAPSULE

TIME CAPSULE

DO NOT OPEN
FOR 500 YEARS

Hundreds of years from now, people are gonna want to know how you lived your life. What kinds of clothes did you wear? What kinds of stuff did you read? What did you do for entertainment?

Fill up a box with things you think will give people in the future a good picture of what you're like. List the things you're gonna put in the box, then bury it where no one will dig it up for a long time!

1.

2.

3.

4.

5.

6.

7.

8.

The BEST JOKE
you ever heard

Five things NOBODY KNOWS about you

BECAUSE THEY NEVER BOTHERED TO ASK

1.

2.

3.

4.

5.

I CAN PUT MY WHOLE FOOT IN MY MOUTH!

YOU'RE GROSS!

The WORST NIGHTMARE
you ever had

TARANTULA
FARM

Rules for your

1. Don't talk to me before 8:00 in the morning.

2. Don't make me sit next to my little brother on spaghetti night.

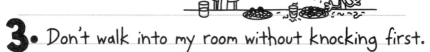

3. Don't walk into my room without knocking first.

4. Don't borrow my underwear under any circumstances.

FAMILY

1.

2.

3.

4.

The SCOOP on your

The person you'd trust to keep
a secret: _____

The person who'd be a good
roommate in college: _____

The person you'd trust to go
clothes shopping for you: _____

The person you'd trust to give
you a haircut: _____

The person who's the worst liar: _____

The person who's most likely to
blame a fart on someone else: _____

The person who's most likely to
borrow something and forget to
give it back: _____

CLASSMATES

The person who'd have the best
chance of surviving in the wild: _____

The person you'd want to do
your homework for you: _____

The person who doesn't have a
"whispering voice": _____

The person you wouldn't want
to get in a fistfight with: _____

The person who you wish lived
in your neighborhood: _____

The person who's most likely to
do something crazy on a dare: _____

The person you really wouldn't
want to get hold of this book: _____

Your life, by

Longest you've ever
gone without bathing:

_____

 Most bowls of cereal you've
ever eaten at one time:

_____

Longest you've ever been grounded: _____

Latest you've ever
been for school:

_____

Number of times you've
been chased by a dog:

_____

 Number of times you've been
locked out of the house:

_____

the numbers

Most hours you've spent
doing homework in one night:

_____

Most money you've ever saved up: _____

Length of the shortest book
you've ever used for a book report:

_____

Farthest distance you've ever walked:

_____

Longest you've ever gone without watching TV:

_____

Number of times
you've gotten caught
picking your nose:

_____

Number of times you've
gotten away with
picking your nose:

_____

Your life, by

Age you were when you
learned to ride a bicycle:

_____

Longest amount of time
you've spent away from home:

_____

Amount of time you spend
watching TV each day:

_____

Age you'd pick if you had to
stay the same age forever:

_____

Number of times you've
watched your favorite movie:

_____

Number of times you've flown in an airplane: _____

the numbers

Most number of times you've
eaten fast food in a single day:

_____

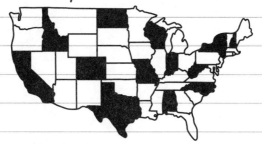

Number of states you've been to: _____

Most pets you've had at one time: _____

Most cavities you've
ever had in one
dental appointment:

_____

Longest you've ever waited in a line: _____

Unfinished

Li'l Cutie

" *Mommy, did my pencil go to heaven?* **"**

Li'l Cutie

" _____ **"**

COMICS

Li'l Cutie

" _____ "

Li'l Cutie

" _____ "

Make your

"   "

OWN comics

66   99

Come up with your own CATCHPHRASE

You know how some character in a movie or a TV show says something funny, and the next thing you know, EVERYONE is saying it? Well, why not come up with your OWN catchphrase, print up a bunch of T-shirts, and totally cash in?

ZOO-WEE MAMA!

BONUS: Come up with another catchphrase and put it on a hat!

In case you get AMNESIA...

People in the movies are always getting clonked on the head, then waking up and not remembering who they are or where they came from. In case that ever happens to you, you should write down the most important facts about yourself now so you can get a head start on getting your memory back!

1.

2.

3.

4.

I PREFER SLEEPING IN RED FOOTIE PAJAMAS!

The FIRST FOUR LAWS you'll pass when you get elected president

1.

2.

3.

4.

" I hereby decree that no middle school student shalt have to take a shower after Phys Ed. "

The BADDEST THING
you ever did as a little kid

Probing

Have you ever eaten food that was in the garbage?

YES ☐   NO ☐

FRIES

Which restaurant do you think makes the best french fries?

_____

What's something you tried once but will never try again?

What's something you wish you were brave enough to do?

_____

If you could eliminate one holiday, which one would you choose?

I ♥ U

_____

QUESTIONS

How old do you think a person should have to be before they get their first cell phone?

_____

What's the most boring sport to watch on TV?

_____

If you could go on a shopping spree at any store, which store would you choose?

_____

If someone wrote a book about your life, what would the title be?

_____

_____

_____

_____

The Sweet Smell of SUCCESS

The Greg Heffley Story

Practice your
SIGNATURE

You'll be famous one day, so let's face it...that signature of yours is gonna need some work. Use this page to practice your fancy new autograph.

List your INJURIES

SKINNED ELBOW
(TRIPPED ON CURB)

PLASTIC SHOE
STUCK UP NOSE

BUSTED CHIN (LEGS FELL
ASLEEP AFTER STAYING ON
THE TOILET TOO LONG)

BITE MARK ON
BACK OF LEG
(FREGLEY)

BROKEN PINKIE
(SLAMMED IN DOOR BY
LITTLE BROTHER)

A few questions

Do you believe in unicorns?

If you ever got to meet a unicorn, what would you ask it?

Have you ever drawn a picture that was so scary that it gave you nightmares?

How many nights a week do you sleep in your parents' bed?

from ROWLEY

Have you ever tied your shoes without help from a grown-up?

Have you ever gotten sick from eating cherry lip gloss?

Are your friends jealous that you're a really good skipper?

Design your own

When you're famous, people are gonna want to name stuff after you. In fact, a few years from now, restaurants could be selling a sandwich with your name on it. So you might as well pick out the ingredients now.

WHITE BREAD

SWISS CHEESE

CHICKEN TENDER

KETCHUP

PEPPERONI

LETTUCE

BARBECUE SAUCE

"The Rowley"

SANDWICH

STACK YOUR SANDWICH HERE

The BIGGEST MISTAKES

1. Believing my older brother when he said it was "Pajama Day" at my school.

2. Taking a dare that probably wasn't worth it.

3. Giving Timmy Brewer my empty soda bottle.

you've made so far

1.

2.

3.

Create your own

TEAM NAME: _____

CITY: _____

SPORT: _____

LOGO:

TEAM MASCOT:

↑ DRAW IT HERE

SPORTS TEAM

STARTING ROSTER

	NAME	POSITION
1.		
2.		
3.		
4.		
5.		

UNIFORM:

Unfinished

Creighton the Cretin

COMICS

Creighton the Cretin

Make your

OWN comics

RODRICK'S

INTELLIGENCE TESTER:

Do this maze and then check to see if you're dumb or smart.

START

FINISH

(If you can finish this, you're smart, and if you can't, you're dumb.)

Put this sentence up to a mirror and then read it as loud as you can:

I AM A MORON.

Fill in the blank below:

Q: Who is awesome?

A: RODR_CK

(Hint: "I")

ACTIVITY PAGES

Answer this question yes or no <u>only</u>:

Q: Are you embarrassed that you pooped in your diaper today?

_____

Do you want to start a band? Well I guess you're out of luck because the best name is already taken and that's Löded Diper. But if you still want to start a band then you can use this mix-and-match thing: *

<u>FIRST HALF</u>	<u>SECOND HALF</u>
Wikkid	Lizzerd
Nästy	Pigz
Vilent	Vömmit
Rabbid	Dagger
Killer	Syckle
Ransid	Smellz

* P.S. If you use one of these names you owe me a hundred bucks.

Form your own

BAND NAME:

GENRE:
(ROCK, POP, RAP, COUNTRY, ETC.)

LOGO →

LEAD SINGER: DRUMMER:

LEAD GUITARIST: BASS GUITARIST:

BAND

Design a poster to advertise your first show!

Write your own

DIPER OVERLÖDE by Rodrick Heffley

We're coming through your speakers
Runnin' through your town
We're pourin' through your headphones
And your eyes are turnin' brown.

We're pumpin' up the volume
And we can't be stopped!
Your brains are leakin' out your ears
Your head's about to pop.

This is a Diper!
A Diper Overlöde.
And you better run for cover
'Cause we're 'bout to explode.

Said it's a Diper!
A Diper Overlöde.
And your mother's gonna shudder
When this Diper hits the road.

The pressure's buildin' up now
And we're about to bust out!
Rockin' stadiums, gymnasiums,
If you're feelin' us, shout!

Yes, it's a Diper!
A Diper Overlöde.
And you ain't been this covered
Since the last time it snowed.

SONG

Design your own

DON'T FORGET BUNK BEDS, COUCHES, A KITCHEN,
A BATHROOM, TELEVISIONS, AND ANYTHING ELSE
YOU'LL NEED FOR LIFE ON THE ROAD!

TOUR BUS

LÖDED DIPER

Plan the ultimate

People to invite

★
★
★
★

Things to pack

★   ★
★   ★
★   ★
★   ★

Music to bring

★   ★
★   ★
★   ★
★   ★

ROAD TRIP

Places to see

★   ★
★   ★
★   ★
★   ★

Map your route

Your DRESSING

If you end up being a famous musician or a movie star, you're gonna need to put together a list of things you'll need in your dressing room.

Requirements for Greg Heffley - page 1 of 9

3 liters of grape soda

2 extra-large pepperoni pizzas

2 dozen freshly baked chocolate chip cookies

1 bowl of jelly beans (no pink or white ones)

1 popcorn machine

1 52-inch plasma TV

3 video game consoles with 10 games apiece

1 soft-serve ice cream machine

10 waffle cones

1 terry-cloth robe

1 pair of slippers

*** bathroom must have heated toilet seat

*** toilet paper must be name brand

ROOM requirements

You might as well get your list together now so that you're ready when you hit the big time.

How well do you

Answer these questions, and then ask your friend the same things. Keep track of how many answers you got right.

FRIEND'S NAME: _____

Has your friend ever gotten
carsick? _____

If your friend could meet any
celebrity, who would it be? _____

Where was your friend born? _____

Has your friend ever laughed
so hard that milk came out
of their nose? _____

Has your friend ever been
sent to the principal's office? _____

9—10: YOU KNOW YOUR FRIEND SO WELL IT'S SCARY
6—8: NOT BAD...YOU KNOW YOUR FRIEND PRETTY WELL!

know your FRIEND?

What's your friend's favorite
junk food? _____

Has your friend ever broken
a bone? _____

When was the last time your
friend wet the bed? _____

If your friend had to
permanently transform into
an animal, what animal would
it be? _____

Is your friend secretly
afraid of clowns? _____

Now count up your correct answers and look at the
scale below to see how you did.

2–5: DID YOU GUYS JUST MEET OR SOMETHING?
0–1: TIME TO GET A NEW FRIEND

Take a friendship

Want to see if you and your friend are a good match? First, go through each pair of items below and circle the one you like best.

COMPATIBILITY TEST

Then have your friend go through the same list and make their selections. See how well your answers match up!

If you had a

If you could go back in time and change the future, but you only had five minutes, where would you go?

If you could go back in time and witness any event in history, what would it be?

If you had to be stuck living in some time period in the past, what time period would you pick?

TIME MACHINE...

If you could go back and videotape one event from your own life, what would it be?

If you could go back and tell your past self one thing, what would it be?

If you could go forward in time and tell your future self something, what would it be?

YOU LOOK RIDICULOUS IN THOSE SOCKS!

FAH!

Totally awesome

The "Stand on One Foot" trick

STEP ONE: On your way home from school, bet your friend they can't stand on one foot for three minutes without talking.

STEP TWO: While your friend stands on one foot, knock real hard on some crabby neighbor's front door.

STEP THREE: Run.

PRACTICAL JOKES

A JOKE YOU'VE PLAYED ON A FRIEND:

A JOKE YOU'VE PLAYED ON A FAMILY MEMBER:

A JOKE YOU'VE PLAYED ON A TEACHER:

Draw your BEDROOM

the way it looks right now

Unfinished

The Amazing Fart Police

COMICS

The Amazing Fart Police

Make your

OWN comics

Your best ideas for

BAD-BREATH DEFLECTOR

ELECTRIC FAN

HEAVY-DUTY ELASTIC STRAP

MR. HHHHHEFFLEY, DO YOU HHHHAVE YOUR HHHHOMEWORK?

WHIRR

ANIMAL TRANSLATOR

HEADSET

COMPUTER PACK

MICRO-PHONE

BARK! BARK! BARK!

HELLO! HELLO! HELLO!

FLAVOR STICK

ROLLING PIN COATED WITH POTATO CHIP FLAVOR DUST

(FLAVOR DUST CAN BE SOUR CREAM AND ONION, CHEDDAR CHEESE, OR BARBECUE)

LICK

INVENTIONS

WRITE DOWN YOUR OWN AWESOME IDEAS
SO YOU CAN PROVE YOU CAME UP WITH
THEM BEFORE ANYONE ELSE.

Design your own
SHOES

Famous athletes have their own custom-designed shoes, so why shouldn't you? Design a basketball shoe and a sneaker that fit your personality.

All-Purpose
EXCUSE MAKER

Did you forget to do your homework? Were you late for school? Whatever the situation, you can use this handy Excuse Maker to get yourself out of a bind. Just pick one item from each column and you're all set!

MY MOTHER	TORE UP	MY HOMEWORK
MY DOG	ATE	MY BUS
MY PINKY TOE	STEPPED ON	MY BEDROOM
A RANDOM GUY	INJURED	MY CLOTHES
THE TOILET	SMACKED	MY LUNCH
A COCKROACH	SMOOSHED	YOUR MONEY

THE TOILET INJURED MY LUNCH!

Make a map of your

GREG HEFFLEY'S NEIGHBORHOOD

N
W · E
S

ROWLEY'S
HOUSE

POND

FREGLEY'S
HOUSE

MY
HOUSE

THE SNELLAS'
HOUSE

WHIRLEY
STREET
KIDS

SHORTCUT

LELAND'S
HOUSE

GRAMMA'S
HOUSE

SCHOOL

HOLLY
HILLS'S
HOUSE

NEIGHBORHOOD

YOUR NEIGHBORHOOD

Make your own

FRONT

Dear Aunt Jean,

THANK YOU

for the wonderful socks you knitted for me.

INSIDE

But next time, could we just stick with cash?

FRONT

I'm sorry

that it didn't work out with you and Lyndsey.

INSIDE

P.S. Could you find out if she thinks I'm "cute"?

GREETING CARDS

FRONT

INSIDE

FRONT

INSIDE

The BEST VACATION
you ever went on

Pearls of WISDOM

Write down great quotes from famous people or from people you know!

FISH AND VISITORS STINK IN THREE DAYS!

NEVER EAT YELLOW SNOW!

UH-OH!

Unfinished

Xtreme Sk8ers

COMICS

Xtreme Sk8ers

THE END

Make your

OWN comics

Design your own

HAUNTED HOUSE

If you had

If you had the power to read other people's thoughts, would you really want to use it?

YES ☐ NO ☐

I WONDER IF MY BAND-AID FELL OFF INTO THAT BAG OF POTATO CHIPS?

CHEW CHEW

CHIPS

If you were a super hero, would you want to have a sidekick?   YES ☐ NO ☐

THANK YOU BOTH FOR SAVING US!

ACTUALLY, IT WAS LIKE 99% ME.

R

SUPERPOWERS...

If you were a super hero, would you keep your identity secret?　YES ☐　NO ☐

Would you want to have X-ray vision if you couldn't turn it off?　YES ☐　NO ☐

Draw your FRIENDS

the way Greg Heffley would

A few questions

Do you ever put food in your belly button so you can have a snack later on?

Do animals ever use their thoughts to talk to you?

Has your guidance counselor ever called you "unpredictable and dangerous"?

from FREGLEY

If you had a tail, what would you do with it?

Have you ever eaten a scab?

Do you wanna play "Diaper Whip"?

Have you ever been sent home from school early for "hygiene issues"?

You probably didn't wipe good enough again, Fregley.

Create your own

Dream up the ultimate competition, then pick the winner! Here's how it works. First, come up with a category for your tournament (Movie Villains, Sports Stars, Cartoon Characters, Bands, Breakfast Foods, TV Shows, etc.)

Then write an entry on each one of the numbered lines. Judge the winner of each individual matchup and move the winner to the next round.

ROUND 1

ROUND 2

ROUND 3

1.

2.

3.

4.

V

TOURNAMENT

For example, in a battle of breakfast foods, you might pick cereal over eggs, so cereal would make it to the next round.

1. CEREAL

CEREAL

2. EGGS

Keep going until only two entries remain. When your final two teams face off, circle the one you think is the best. That's your winner!

ROUND 1

ROUND 2

ROUND 3

5.

6.

7.

8.

S.

Autographs

What do you see in these

Take a look at these inkblots and write down what you think they look like. You'll have to use your imagination! What you see in these inkblots probably says something about your personality... but it's up to you to decide WHAT!

INKBLOTS?

TWO TURTLES PLAYING TENNIS!

135

The FIRST CHAPTER

Chapter One
CHILDHOOD

I was born in _____ on _____, _____. I was ____ inches long and _____ pounds, and I looked like a _____.

I spent my first few months doing a lot of _____ and _____, until I was ____ months old and I finally started to _____.

From a very early age, I had a talent for _____, but I never really got the hang of _____. I liked to eat _____, but I never could stand _____.

When I turned ____, I started to get really interested in _____, but I got bored with that when I turned ____ and moved on to _____ instead.

# of your AUTOBIOGRAPHY

As a little kid, I was brave enough to
_____, but I was
scared to death of _____.
In fact, to this day, I won't go near a _____
_____.

My best friend growing up was a kid named
_____, who now works as a
_____ in _____.
My most treasured possession as a kid was a
_____. My best birthday
party was when I turned _____ and I got a new
_____ from _____.

My favorite TV show was _____
_____, and when I wasn't
watching television, I'd _____
_____ for hours at a time.

When I was a little kid, everyone always told
me that one day, I'd grow up to become a
_____. Who knew that I'd
actually become a _____?

ZOO-WEE MAMA by Rowley

Gareth the GREEN BEAN

by Fregley

Gareth is an ordinary student who just so happens to be a green bean.

Gareth
(actual size)

Gareth's classmates are always picking on him because he's so small.

Hey, you're sittin' in my seat!

I don't see your name on it.

It's about to have a little green stain on it.

Gareth tries out for sports but doesn't have a lot of luck.

Look at what's hangin' out of my nose, fellas!

Unhand me, you fiend!

HA HA HA

HA HA HA

JEROME

the man with
INCREDIBLY
RED LIPS

BY GREG HEFFLEY

THE AMAZING FART POLICE

by Greg Heffley

CONGRATULATIONS GRADUATES

We're so proud of you, Joey!

Thanks, Aunt Lydia!

Whup!

HUG

TOOT

FART POLICE!

You're under arrest!

But it wasn't my fault! My aunt squeezed it out of me!

FP FP

Tell it to the judge, kid.

FP

CLICK

FART POLICE! Put your hands in the air.

I thought public restrooms were free-fart zones!

FP FP

Ignorance of the law is no excuse.

FP

CLICK

NEXT WEEK: THE FART POLICE INVADE A BURRITO FACTORY

ACTION FIGHTERZ by Rowley

TOMORROW: LOOK OUT!

TOMORROW: PAIN!

THE STORY SO FAR...

KAPTAIN KLOBBER IS ABOUT TO CLONK MR. PUNCHO UPSIDE THE HEAD WITH A SKILLET.

TOMORROW: IMPACT!

NEXT WEEK: MR. PUNCHO HITS BACK!

TURN THE PAGE! ➡

Gareth the GREEN BEAN in

GARETH'S REVENGE

by Fregley

One day, a letter arrives in the mail for Gareth...

What's this?

Dear Gareth,

You have been chosen to attend the Greenwarts School of Wizards and Warlocks!*

* which is in no way affiliated with the Hogwarts School of Witchcraft and Wizardry

Take that, you fiends!

AIEEEEEEEEEEE!

ZAP

Hmm...

Precious Poochie

by Eldridge Perro

Office Antix

by Bert Salas

Oh, Grampsie!

by Beverly Bliss

Dear Diary,
Today I spent my allowance money on a gift for Greg. He is my very best friend in the whole wide world so I got a locket we could both wear to make it official.

It turns out Greg doesn't really like jewelry, but I'm still gonna wear my half.

Maybe Greg is still mad at me for what I did Saturday when I slept over at his house.

He caught me in the bathroom trying on his retainer, and he yelled at me for ten whole minutes.

Sometimes Greg gets frustrated with me and calls me bad names, but I don't mind too much. I still know I'm an awesome, friendly kid because my mom and dad are always telling me so.

Dear Diary,
 I sure am glad to have Greg as my best friend because he is always giving me tips about school. Like today he told me the boys' and girls' locker rooms in the gym were labeled wrong.

Well, it turns out Greg got his facts mixed up on that one.

SCREAM!!!

I got sent to the principal's office and after that I found Greg to tell him the doors weren't labeled wrong after all.

Greg actually makes those kinds of mistakes a <u>lot</u>. Last year Greg told me the next day was pajama day at school, and it turns out he was wrong.

Luckily Greg forgot to wear his pajamas to school so he didn't get embarrassed too.

Sometimes Greg is a little grouchy, but I am always doing things to cheer him up.

So now you can see why me and Greg are such good pals and why we will always be

Create your own COVER

DIARY

of a

What's YOUR story?

Use the rest of this book to keep a daily journal, write a novel, draw comic strips, or tell your life story.

But whatever you do, make sure you put this book someplace safe after you finish it.

Because when you're rich and famous, this thing is gonna be worth a FORTUNE.

SECURITY

ABOUT THE AUTHOR

(THAT'S YOU)

ACKNOWLEDGMENTS

(THE PEOPLE YOU WANT TO THANK)